The Path

by Debbie Shapiro
illustrated by Tim Jones

Harcourt

Orlando   Boston   Dallas   Chicago   San Diego

Visit *The Learning Site!*

www.harcourtschool.com

"Where is the path?"
asked Jill.

She could use help.
Friends could help.

Ben thinks.
Ben steps with his
new boots.

4

Then Jill could step
where Ben did.

That will help her!
Ben stomps a path.

"Thanks!" said Jill.
"Now I can put my
steps where you did."

We can all use this
path of steps.